Flames of the Moon

ANURAG CHALLAPALLI

First Published in March 2020

ISBN: 978-93-90030-02-6

BLUEROSE PUBLISHERS
www.bluerosepublishers.com
info@bluerosepublishers.com
+91 8882 898 898

Cover Design:
Tyngshain Pariat

Typographic Design:
Ayushi Garg

Distributed by: BlueRose, Amazon, Flipkart, Shopclues

Preface

Love is the most exceptional feeling in anyone's life. It starts with parents, family, and friends. Like a river that travels all the way, at last, it finds the ocean. One day someone will come into our life. They become very special to us, and our hearts beat for them. It bleeds for them. It quests for them. It suffers from them, and It fights for them, it lives for them, and finally, it dies for them even. It is beyond a four-letter word, and sometimes words are not enough to express. Besides, it is not also enough to store in our small heart.

I started writing poetry 18 years back. I wanted to build an empire with the words of every lover on this planet. The greatest tragedy in one's life is living without or beloved presence. Separation is not for two people, it is for two souls. When we come to know that we should live without the one who is the only one for us, it is like living with half heart. Each second passing without them is like dying every second. This book is the passion of true love. This book is the BIBLE of people who are mad for their loved ones. This book is the anthem for the one who is living with half hearts. Loving is like discovering selfless happiness. To be loved is getting an enormous privilege. If you don't have that, you can still live happily. Poetry is the language of love. Poetry is an expression of our deeper feelings, shortly and simply. I tried with the best of my abilities to make people understand it efficiently and effectively.

Poetry generates an enormous feeling in a few words. It inspires us. It requires that grand splendour of expression conveyed in simple language. Every word should be right, and pleasant words should deeply penetrate in our hearts. The poets are they who see this world differently. It is beyond imagination. That rule the world.

Poets must reach like the sky is the limit, and even above that, the poet must not only express pure thoughts, but he must demonstrate it to even a layman to feel its senses. His words must be pictures. The meaning of poems must hold as absolute truth.

This book is the work of pure love and pain of a lover living alone in the absence of beloved. Love is not a cakewalk. It is a walk on roses with thorns. This book demonstrates the beauty of love as we see the beauty in a rose as well as the pain of love we get in separation and breakup as the thorns we see in the rose plant.

About the Author

Anurag Challapalli is an MBA Graduate. By Profession, he is a User Experience Designer from Hyderabad. Anurag has designed several web and mobile applications for various sectors like Manufacturing, E-Commerce, Hospitality, and Engineering sectors. His first book, *Flames of the Moon*, is about Love and separation.

Acknowledgements

I took nearly 18 years to complete this book. Since my childhood, I got the inspiration to write from R.K Narayan's *Malgudi Days* which had a profound influence on me. Great legendary director, K.Viswanath sir movies, also had a significant impact on me. It created more interest for me to write. I had a passion for writing, but I don't have a proper approach and enough skills. A relative of mine is the only person who encouraged me all the way. In this journey, Perry Poetry Quotes and Eric Hanson Poems and Quotes influenced me in several ways to write all stages of love.

Dedication

I thank my parents and family for their support and faith in me· I will always work to keep up their respect·

I will be lifelong thankful to the one and only person who encouraged me from the beginning· I will never forget the support I have got·

This book is the work of true love· This book is a platform for me to show respect and gratitude to my beloved person· I dedicated this book to "Junnu·"

Author Signature

Contents

You're the One

You are the one... From the shining stars to Series of my classic moments. You are the one ...From the colours of Sunrise to the Journey of my desires.

You are the one... From the spaces between my fingers to the holding coffee cups waiting for you. You are the one... From the sound of my heartbeat to the tears of my long wait.

You are the one... From the trees, which hugs me with their soft arms to the air, bounces back from you like a wave. You are the one from the secret meetings in the mornings to the nights passed away without you alone.

You are the one ...From the dance of rose petals to the wounds that narrate tales of my misery. You are the one ...From my smile beside your stand and desperate wait for your touch.

You are the one ...From the depths of ocean blues to the peaks of your desire fastens my heartbeat. You are the one ...From your eyes which produces a story of a lifetime to the true definition of beauty.

You are the one ...From the roadmap to miracles, hidden in your eyes, to the kisses on my bruises, take my pain away. You are the one ...From the gateway to the roads of the mystic city. You had the magic of turning on lights of your charm in my endless love.

My Heartbeat is you

In the coldest nights, I want to wrap my arms around you tight – when silence is striking us terrifying. You're that part of me I always needed. I heard the sweetest sound of my life, your heartbeat.

I quickly lose control over myself when I hug you from your back, and I still never know the way to come out. Your eyes lock my heart. I drown in your looks, every drop of your love-filled my lungs.

The very moment you leave me, I start replaying our conversations. I wonder what will happen when we meet next time. But I promise you the very moment you come back to me; I will kiss you from head to toe to tell you much I missed you.

In your tough times, I will hold your face gently to say that if you have my eyes, I would be able to show you how much you are important to me. You are precious than anything in this world. You are everything for me for the next 10 million years.

My heart no longer knew that one day it would happen. But when it happened, it seemed everything stopped. Is this meant to last long, killing me every second? Even when death is embracing me. I see my life in you, and I will leave my heartbeat for you.

A Princess in my Breath

She brought me to the places I had never been to before. In the evenings at the hillside, she glowed like the red moon. Her magic made me her disciple. Her presence made me her devotee. Finally, she made me belong to her.

She came like a star falling from the sky. Even after eras of separation shattered me, I will still feel her somewhere in a milky way. Finally, she came with the gift of a lifetime, and she came with word of an everlasting promise, which ended my long wait.

She smiled at me from a letter enclosed in an envelope. I didn't send that. Inside that letter, I wrote the story of a moon, about how she left me, night after night darkness occupied me. I spent those days in mourning and dying every day.

She stuns my world full of puzzles that I love to solve. Inside me, I was fragile that I could barely stand up. Her magnifying touch gives a tremendous amount of energy, and she brings me closer to the impossible conclusion that I never knew it would happen.

Hiding You in My Poetry

My heart mourned in the cold and had no desire to change. I'd remain the same without any change, and I lacked vision in my life. A belief arose gently.

It seemed I felt no longer fit in anything. The world is changing every day except me. In those stringent times, you stood for me. You guided me as a dearest friend. You guarded me as my mother. From that moment, I started admiring your heart. I love to drown in it because you hold a fantastic spot of beauty.

In the rotten parts of my desert, you grow roses giving hope for tomorrow. You rolled those rose petals on the sand. I stood as a spectator of your magic when you turned the dusty desert into shining pearls. You hold my hand and taught me your spell, I don't have any words to write, that I could ever imagine.

You made me hear the voices of the lifetime, and on the strangest seas, I began the voyage to the tail of comets. There you directed winds to play celestial lullabies.

You are my universe, and your lips became my language. Every stretchmark on your skin narrated the tales of Angels. You became my million volumes of a lifetime.

Life can be a combination of sunshine and rainbows. Days beside you passed like seconds. In your absence, my heart squeezed with pain, and my tears threw me in hell.

I am from nowhere and belong to none. You took me to somewhere and made me yours. When you carried me inside yourself, and I always hide you in my poetry.

A Night of Angel Sleep

When your beloved people surrounded you like multiple tornadoes, like gentle rain, you glowed like diamonds on the snow. Let your awakenings in the morning quiet the rush of birds.

Storms tore your nerves apart. When your steps do not move forward, let the jasmines hold you tight, and the roses talk to might. My hands turn into feathers, let me take you to the flight. On the Moon, I will make your bed.

Loads of weights pressing your shoulders down to the ground. I wish the windows of your bedroom play the music of my feelings and rabbits to sing the lyrics of my concepts. Join me on the top of your roof, let my princess breathe the breeze of my love.

When life tied you up in chains when all took you for granted, may the pages in my book dare to say you are a line of infinite and a place which leads to the gateway of miracles.

In the nights, you can't close your eyes when your thoughts were too deep. When your mind walked out of silence and fallen, may the stars from the sky drop into your lap. Let the snow calm your worries. Let me be your dance through the threads of your bed sheet.

Your words described reality, and my eyes knew that you are waiting for a start. Let me take you for a walk on the hillside. Let me take you on the top of your tears. I will put you on the world's safest place, that is my heart.

Craving about u

I crave you in my words that adores you.

I crave you in my soul that worship you.

I crave you in my arms that unite us together.

I crave you in my eyes, which changed the view of the universe which I used to see earlier.

I crave you in the flowers shining in the sunsets and move across all the things that stretch to infinity.

I crave for your palm, and I wish to see that carved on my heart.

I crave for you to carry you with me forever.

In Your Absence

Seconds filled with your absence. You released a beast out of me. I was wondering what would happen. Slowly in the night. At world's end, I opened the gates of my desires to conquer every inch of you. My concepts come out of our dark fantasies. In the end, we started penetrating each other in a mad passion.

Minutes were passing with your absence. Fate threw stones on me. I carried those stones and wrote my stories on it. And when I read those chapters, I remember every step I had walked with you.

Days were passing with your absence, and you light the fireworks in my heart. This world seems broken. In my thoughts, I released butterflies of your voice to conquer the shores of paradise.

Weeks were passing with your absence. You tore me into pieces. The dark storm carried me, and wild winds shook me in the truth of how deeply you had penetrated inside me.

Months were passing with your absence. You turned my blood into lava bursting out of my veins. I sailed right down to the place where you blended as a hurricane.

Life passing with your absence turned me still in silence. No matter what happens to embrace your presence, I will wait like a golden water drop. One day I will have your perfume of you

what you had left for me.

Counting on Stars

In the thoughts of you, counting on stars for another trillion seconds, I am in another day. Slowly, I discovered myself through your feelings.

In dreams of you, hundreds of the ages I travelled on the tail of comets, to find a place that could match your smile.

In the memories of you, a beautiful sunrise whispered to the wind, wrote a song with pearls to shine through you.

In the presence of you, never could I paint a rose, when I realized, you are rose garden's planet I am walking through it.

In your anger, deep in my heart, you froze me in shocking surprises, I am craving to melt in your hot desires.

In the writings of you, remembering that you're not poetry I made. You're just a beautiful creation that rolled through my mind.
In the world of you, it became inevitable, watching you is the same feeling as the king of this world. You are my angel; I could see and worship you forever.

In the absence of you, knowing death can tear me apart from you, I am a proud man to end my life. I remember that I have lived in the time of you.

In life you, always and evermore, life is a gift, but you made it a miracle for me.

Falling in Love all with You

I don't know why I fell in love with you. When did I start asking myself why I fell in love with you? Nonetheless, I didn't get any answer. Then I started writing a list of everything I fell in love with you.

I fell in love with your amazing looks.

I fell in love with your eyes that light up my mine and awakes me in the morning.

I fell in love with your smile that fastens my heartbeat.

I fell in love with your whisper that hugs my soul.

I fell in love with your expressions at me. It makes me a mad bull.

I fell in love with your lovely chat with me that gives wings for me to fly.

I fell in love with your unseen wounds.

I fell in love with your ways of becoming part of me.

I fell in love with your lovely stretch marks.

I fell in love with your inspiring fight in tougher times.

I fell in love with your tears came out of when you left isolated for the last decade.

I fell in love with your fear of losing me.

I fell in love with your ways that you find to ignore me.

I fell in love with your extreme anger for me.

I fell in love with your methods of torturing me.

Knowing that I am in love

I know I am in love when I can feel my arms hold you tight after the long years, you left me.

I know I am in love when I can still feel the taste of your lips after years of your touch.

I know I am in love when the feeling of tearing apart in my heart. The truth that I am not going to be with you.

I know I am in love when you are beside me, you heal me as a medicine, and you turn me into a garland to worship you.

I know I am in love when I hear your name, my spine setbacks beyond the skies.

I know I am in love. You are the only person I always think about, breathe, and live, but you are away from me.

I know I am in love when your tears wet your eyes, but it is my heart that weeps.

I know I am in love when I go to the place where we walked, I stood there and madly laughed even when you weren't there to walk with me.

I know I am in love when a simple message of you tunes my mind, and my heart composes a beautiful song.

Ultimately, I am in love, and I am living without you.

I know, I am in love. Without you, there is nothing in my life. With you, there are a million stories to write where it was supposed to last for a lifetime.

The word You

Maybe you have mixed feelings for me but remember that I am the one who completes your world that no one ever has. You are the one that I didn't expect in my life. Meeting you was my fate. Falling in love with you is my destiny.

When you notice everything in this world crashing you down, I will stand by your side, keeping you behind me. I will fight with the demons chasing you to let you down when I win this battle for you. I will make you my princess and I will make sure that the entire world come under your feet.

When you roam around the places without my company, I wish time had fixed a different time for you and me. I will take you to the areas that you had never been to show you something that you had never seen. But I would like to tell you that you are way more beautiful than everyplace we had been.

When you don't hear anything from me, it is not that I am not thinking about you. Waiting for your presence beside me and wanting your touch is always my priority. I am away from you, but every memory of you mesmerize me, and I remain silent due to the magic happening in my head.

The Four-letter word

It aches when my eyes refuse to watch you leave. But it will adore you for everything because nothing else mattered.

It breaks in the loneliness but beats to pair with you.

It cracks in silence but craves to have a chat with you.
It mourns in the absence of your hug, but it melts when your shadow left in my arms, and I will never let it go.

It weeps with wounds of long waits but wakes for every chance to be with you.

It was isolated even when surrounded by the world's attention, but it will unite this world just for a small smile of you.
It fears everything which separates you from me, but it will fight with the death to win your presence.

What is it? It is just a four-letter word that rolled out from my mind.

It is a feeling of forever, which took birth in my heart.

About Loving You

Loving you is like a one-time miracle of a lifetime, for you made up like the cause of admiration.

You are a masterpiece. You are one of its kind, and your eyes bring countless miracles that light my darkness.

When you kissed me on the forehead, you exploded a volcano in my heart. I preserved those moments turned into chocolate when you got a piece of it. You made my day.

Everything for you, I might not have said those four magical words, in a way you never even know, I poured my desire over the clouds that I held for you in my intensities of rain.

The moment you passed before me is like kissing an express train. Everything I miss you is more than anything, and I would like to tell you that I'm tired of waiting. I became very desperate to see the moment that you will come back for me, and at that time, I'll say those four magical words.

Until you stroke my face with your hard slap, I swore that these memories were kind I'd always keep.

Near your feet, I left a letter with rose petals that turned into silver when I came back to you in the evening. You took me to the stars and introduced me to them.

Neat and clean the breeze of your touch blows me away, I keep your fragrance and dance like a ghost.

You kept the leaves sing for you on their branches, and your voice speaks someday without hesitation. I realize nothing changes.

Soulmate from my left

You're my soulmate from my left.
Let me put my thoughts on you. That is the way only I feel right.

You're my soulmate from my left.
Let me hold you tight. Let me take you to the heights of my love.

You're my soulmate from my left.
Let me take you to heaven's gate. Please don't leave my hand me in the dark.

You're my soulmate from my left.
Let me tell you are the one who lifts me to the might.

You're my soulmate from my left.
Every night when I open my eyes, the truth that you are not with me is so real.

You're my soulmate from my left.
Each touch of you cracks my breath.
Until the end of my life, you are my soulmate.

You Take my Breath Away

In my dream, you were dressed like a goddess, carrying a magic wand. In the golden light, you glowed like an answer to all my questions. You took my breath away.

When I walk on the road behind you, you leave the air, which hugs me in silence – taking my breath away.

You are a burning sun that I gazed upon. You drew flames of honey on my heartbeat, taking my breath away.

Jasmine's rolling on the ocean bed. With Thunders and hurricanes, you lighten the sparks in the sky. You take my breath away.

Full Moon passing through you, beating the speed with flames melting me softly. You take my breath away.

Mystery's destiny is driving me to the peaks of madness. Your essence made me taste the pearls. You took my breath away.

The Love we have

We have the love where entire universe knew about it. You removed my painful dreams with your magical touch.

Though you keep on hiding from me, the moon finds you; at last, we met in a place meant for us only, and finally, only two of us were there. In my imaginations, I wish to remain with you, and I hope I would never come from it.

The moment I walked with you, I cherish those steps deep in my heart, and I will preserve those moments.

On the high mountains and miles together, we walked... My song will change the weather and that magic showers on you.

Even after my death, my soul's conversation with you will never end. Instead, it will capture you from heaven and above. While I'll burn in hell to protect you. Finally, I will rise again from the ashes to reach you.

Times journey passes on with your shadows... My time froze and stood up on me like a pillar to see the sight of your eyes open in the morning.

Colors of You

It is a privilege to see the sunrise in the early mornings turning into gold when it rises on your feet. The moment you open your eyes, you quicken my pulse rate to the peaks.

Your waiting cheeks to turn red in the evening, like millions of roses in a garden. Those flowers took me for a walk with all the memories of you and me; thorns of separation surrounded me.

Whistles that drizzles a breeze from your busy hands turn to orange. I will feel your breeze in the range of mountain peaks.

Ceasing conversations coming from your lips turns into blue. I will meet you across the stars and stare at you when you are in Infront of me.

Twists and turns taking the edge of your steps turn into green. I will walk with you over the planet of pearls.

Away from you

A cyclone is striking towards me with jet speed. I will be a soldier of your silence to fight with the distances that separated us. I will protect you in every vulnerable situation that terrifies you.

I am living with loneliness without your presence beside me. You plant a seed inside me, and I don't think it will survive. I felt that it would never grow. You always live there, nurturing me inside. But the truth is, it produces the most beautiful flowers.

Walking from east to west, seeing the sunrise to sunsets, knowing that I am human with ten fingers and ten toes, I don't even have a single reason to tell about my goddess turned away from me. Still, my lungs will breathe, my heart will bleed, my eyes will see, and that I always worship you in all uncertain conditions.

When consequences build walls around me, it stood like mountains. You have come like a lifetime promise. Writing poetry on you is covering every inch of you with words I've learned to dress you in the material of my love.

I was carrying the scars and wounds deep inside my heart. I looked for your rays of shine on me and your rain of love on me. To the millionth degree or the other, nothing drowned me blindly as you have done to me.

Holding You Tight

How holding you tight can heal? I will kiss you in a way that my lips say how I feel for you. Take me inside you as we meant for each other.

Our souls will bond; there is no question of promises between us. Our love is itself a promise of a lifetime.

I have written stories of your flaws. I have arranged each one of them like a chain of pearls. I didn't organize them to look beautiful. They describe my situation when I finally found you.

I know I am not unique. I know I cannot see you all the time, but please know that when your days burn you more than anything, I am the one who changes your hot days into a cool breeze.

You asked thousands of questions. And my only answer to you is. You are my masterpiece that I always die to stare at you.

Known Stranger

We are two complicated personalities, but we refused to give up on each other. We danced for the soundtrack of jazz music. A sharp-edged arrow passed between us tore our wide apart.

In the longest nights of cold winters, I sent a question to the might, asking how all this changed trapping me in an unknown place.

It has been a very long time since you disappeared from my sight. I packed the memories with you and ran into the darkness. On the hillside near the jasmine garden, I heard your name called.

My heart roared with a wow. I searched for you in the shadows. You are nowhere that I could find. My restless soul revolted to tear my mourning.

In the monsoon evenings, when my eyes clicked on your lips, your eyes opened windows of the room where I housed. Fate threw thorns on us and signs of separation created deep wounds inside me.

When problems raised curtains on us, we forcibly broke the promises made. Shattered dreams made our hearts filled with tears, but the memories left behind to make us close. We slowly passed without a glimpse as known strangers.

To Dear You

The thoughts you held within for me, I've had painted you with my colours. My words occupy this world but left unexplored, feelings which I cannot show you. I have hidden underneath my feet.

Times that turned into darkness, where I don't dare to go.

From your eyes to the end of your toes, it was still the remain the same. My heart goes crazy about you.

Seeing you is like the sky was the dead-end of my sight, stepping away from you is the fierce wind of the ocean tide.

I keep going beyond galaxies the moment I feel about you every time, it is merely magic, and it was still the same when I was left alone with your absence.

Waves of your hair. You carved in the edges of my blood. The grey of your absence sprinkled poison on me.

Words you speak for me, I turned them into gold in the monsoon season.

My heart no longer knew, then one day this happened, I will write this poetry till my last breath.

Thorn in my Heart

There you stood still like an angel with wings. Waving back to you, I feared the moment dreaming about you. You tied my arms tight, throwing me to the distances fall on me apart.

Streets spread with my love letters near your house. I sat on a bench, waiting for you to come out of the balcony. Loneliness gave me the company. I became eager to see your gestures. And I searched for every possibility of you, to stay beside me.

On the seashore in the wet sands, I searched in every grain, finding a probability that you might have walked on it. When ocean tides slowly rolled on my feet, I heard the music of sad symphony. I started singing the lyrics of the pain you gave me.

Slowly a picture rolled in my mind that you texted me with words of honey. Over the moon, in darkness, you left me. I see nothing but my tears whispered the words of agony.

When you abandoned me, my heart knew that the truth you are not mine. It cracks with disappointment, it breaks with agony, and it is writhing in pain. In the end, when you call my name, I lose control over myself. I will be with you.

My love has a curse of beauty, and it doesn't know that it will be plucked out like a beautiful flower, leaving no chances to flourish. But then you did it. You have not stopped with that. Instead, you planted a thorn in my heart, leaving me in vain.

You are My Garden

I closed my eyes and walked into the garden without any sense of feel.

The very first thing I heard was the music of birds. Then I danced with bliss. It happens when I hear my name from you.

I moved inside with a thirst for loneliness. Where the buzz of bees on the lotus helped me to quench my thirst, I felt my nerves moving apart. It happens when I come closer to you.

I sat on a bench for a while. When conversations of rabbits led my way to them, they fell on me to wish. It made my blood flow like a waterfall. It happened when your lips met mine.

I stretched my hands. I moved further. Beautiful jasmines and its fragrance turned me mad. It happened when I felt low in disappointment. You took me into your lap and gave me the strength to fight.

Then I finally opened my eyes to search for you, late at night, I looked over the sky above me. Full moon and stars were glowing like a miracle on me. I spoke to the moon to convey a message to you. You are my moon that makes me shine in this world.

Thinking about you makes me forget everything. You occupy my thoughts every day and night. Everything about you is something I have. And I wanted to let you know that you are the one that my soul lives on.

Mad Wind

In the evening, restlessness drew flames of distress on me. You wiped my tears with a smile bringing colourful breezes. I was a disease, and you have become a cure.

I was watching you from distances while climbing the steps to open heaven's door. Parrots narrated me tales of your voices. Squirrels took me to the golden cradle where you slept. Finally, I became the poetry slipped from your fingers, describing every wonder of you.

You mould me with your magical eyes, you made me with the flares of your smile, and you showed me the flavour of your actions. You had driven me through the airs of thunderbolts.

One way or the other, one life or the other
You are a priceless grace that stuns me all the time. In the nights of cloudless calms and scary skies, all above that, I want to meet you for a few minutes.

When my tears come out from the silence that you had left me, it is a surprise to see them like millions of pearls falling from the sky. Don't delay even for a second; collect them because they are priceless. Store them because they are precious. Would you care for them? because they will narrate sensational stories.

There is a lot of stuff that I would like to talk about you. Can you hold my conversation with your kisses? When I bring my intensity to you. Pain teaches me the act of fate.

Dry my eyes with your lips and slowly whisper in my ears, "Learn to live alone... I am not going to be part of your life but remember, and you're not alone."

Spending Nights in Your Absence

I never stop thinking about you. I am left alone but not living in loneliness.

I am waiting for your love far from the distances. My heart gets goose bumps from your warm breaths.

I wish in the future twists our fate, and happiness bells ring outside our doors. I search for you at night. Waiting for your magic remains me like a statue, even in the hard winds.

You have penetrated the deepest parts of me. But your words treated me very poorly. I had never suffered like this before.

Corner of a florist shop. I was waiting for you holding a bunch of flowers. When you came to me, I just didn't believe that is it real. I told myself not to react, but my passion for you took me to you without any delay.

My love will come to you someday or the other. Please know that you are the only hope of everything I have.

Abandoned Love

Like a wink, the amount of time that we've spent passed. But I will have a library of books for every minute of yours with me. Every time I write a chapter, the idea comes from your company.

You are the most favorite writer of my life. When you started narrating your stories to me by listening to them, I built an empire for you.

When I heard that monsters ripped your thoughts, I'd like to let you know that I will protect you in my arms until the fragrance of happiness embraces your world.

When you show me your scars, I will not step aside. I will heal them with my love. Just like they never existed. All I need from you is a cute smile so that I will glow brightly in it.

A series of frightening consequences can never keep me losing; remember that I will choose you even if your life falls apart.

Remember me even if you caused grave injuries deep inside me, but another way you are still the reason, my pen writes about passion for you.

You travel on the oceans more often; your voyage is not so smooth when a terrible cyclone with a mad storm feared you. When you see the highest waves ahead raising on you like a mountain, remember that I am the one who will join in drowning with you.

If your journey with life goes on, I will exist watching you.

Favorite Seconds with You

My favourite seconds with you...

The seconds when...
Your actions complete me. Even though my visions destroyed, I remain to believe a celebration will come for us. It is a very unpleasant situation for me to digest the fact of being without you. Life pulls me down. But still, you are the reason again I will stand up.

The seconds when...
It was a sensation, and it was a lovely tale. It was a golden period when our hearts came closer and smiled as one. That moment stars twinkled under our feet.

The seconds when...
Your words described nothing, but my eyes understood everything. It is your magic made me discover hidden places inside me. You carried ocean of secrets that I love to explore.

The seconds when...
When I lifted you and started kissing intensely, the winds drove your hair to write my name. We laughed until we cried. When your lips moved on my forehead, my heart understood your feelings for me. Then we cried until we laughed.

The seconds when...
My broken heart and my tears make me stronger. But at the end of the day, I still don't know the reason why your presence holds everything that my heart quests.

Broken Rose

I am not who I've been. I've seen the stars burning in the sky and its ashes floating on the water. I have been waiting for you since a very long time, but I am frozen, you are the one who melts me in a countless number of desires.

I am on my way to reach you. But stones blocked me in the way. I stood still cherishing the moments when you taught birds to sing. I spoke with flowers and told them that you are the first one that made me smile.

You held priceless beauty in your eyes. I see my universe within your shadow, and we met where the end begins. It was very natural; the way I feel for you is like an easy way of running crazy.

I will be the broken rose with thorns cut me in bleeding. Still, I will shower fragrance on you. I conquer myself in loving you. When pain breaks me into pieces for the fact, not being part of your life, I still believe that one-day my love shines on you.

Every part of me will be in love with you for the rest of your life. I wanted to be the one that you never see coming. It is tough to believe that you let me go. You may see a million sunrises in my absence, but only I can make that beautiful for you.

Queen on the Shores

There is an empire that exists. She doesn't know about it. When she is asleep, winds slipped through her window and revealed the secrets of a Queen.

Far from here above, clouds were surpassing blue skies. Sun released the sonnets of my fire. It embraced a mighty asteroid, releasing flames and slowly conquered the moon.

From the flames of the moon to the deep ocean blues on the earth, is her kingdom. She walked in her territory on the path of diamonds while lions guarded her with the shields of stars.

On the planet, Neptune angels weaved material for her dress. On Uranus, it is the turn of aliens to add colours to it.

On Saturn, the goddess came from heaven, stitched it with a platinum needle. Jupiter added pearls with golden dust. Deep in the cores of Mars, tigress took the magical wand.

With all the flowers on the Earth added fragrance to her coat. There is a workshop on Venus. Squirrels designed her head crown with Titanium.

When sparks from the sun passed through Mars, those sparks melted iron, which made her sword. Finally, eight planets lined up in one direction to see her crowned on the throne.

On the shores of her kingdom, she slowly walked towards the throne. Ocean tides shouted slogans of pride, and sands chanted her name.

When she decorated the throne, I was just seeing her eyes. There is a world for me in her smile. My queen walked on the shores for me. Then she opened her eyes in the morning.

Want to be a Poem of You

I want to be a poem that will never escape from my magic.

It doesn't matter if I don't see you again. I will bear this pain. When you feel alone, come outside your balcony and see once. I have sent parrots to deliver you the colours which you had painted on my heart.

Like a flower flowing on the ocean of honey, I will flow with the essence of smell and sweetness of your touch.

My thoughts are reflections of you. When my eyes wake up searching for you, in your absence, my tears dry, but the pain drowns.

I was irony long back, but not now. You were the fire that melted me. It had harrowed me when you left me. If tomorrow brings a change, I want that change to be with you.

When You Came Deep into My Heart

I don't know when you came rushing into my breath. I couldn't control that moment. You began to penetrate my living gently.

All I know is you are everywhere. You occupy my every second of thoughts. I lose myself quickly when I walk with you on the streets.

Early in the mornings, holding coffee cups together and carrying memories of hot afternoons at the end of the day when you stepped into my room, I felt you in me.

I get to see you all day around when I work seriously or sit alone with no thinking. All of a sudden, you surprise me with your touch.

I spread the fragrance of your air over my body when I start walking in your path. I started playing your music and my abandoned heart paired with that.

I felt the touch of your lips when I keep waking every night with no hope for tomorrow. Then slowly, you activated my body, my blood, and nerves — every inch of mine.

I don't know how it happened or when it happened. I am living your life with my body and soul.

Life is a jail without you

I am living in jail – my hands are tied, and I welcomed the pain.
I am locked in a cell, where I hardly see any light.
My legs can barely move a step. It doesn't have any scope to progress.
Yes, my jail is a living hell, where I live without my goddess in front of me.
My heart takes pain, where my mind makes stress. But people around smile at me, seeing my tears rolling down in vain.
My work happens due to force. My food doesn't taste, but my eyes don't become wet. Instead, it holds back its place.
My walks keep its rhythm where there are no lyrics written. I see nothing but sky watching at me.
I am having a cup of tea. It doesn't reduce my agony, which my heart is bearing for years. Every sip I take, it starts burning inside.
What happened to me? What is going in my life?
My life is a small room, even when you take my lips on to yours, but without your presence beside me, this world is a jail for me.
My life is two chairs on a balcony. When I see you in the sunset, these days are not getting killed. It is just taking its birth.
My walk keeps the rhythm of music when you wait on the beach, waving towards me to join you.
My food tastes fantastic when you text a simple message to me.
I will have my tea when you join me to take a sip of it. You lift me over the top of the rainbow.
My tears will come out of my eyes when you tell that magical four-letter words to me.
Life is a jail without you.

Definition of Her Tears

You shine with a soft glaze, rainbows cutting your throat, chasing demons of your anguish and breaking the darkness in the tougher times. Roaring cries of the volcano. You rise from the top of the Everest. You turn into fire.

The war of squirrels and flowers in the hurricane. Musician playing a smooth orchestra in the magical winds. Beautiful choruses of a Cinderella, Laid path towards utopia.

Whistles were breaking the silence of her destiny. In the blue seas, she was sleeping in a cradle guarded by moonlight. When green hills blessed with her footsteps and the corals dipped in honey. She drew her magic and led everything with her into a paradise.

Carrying You Inside Me

You didn't say it is over, but you acted like it is the end of our relationship. You are my first love. You are the accomplishment of my life. When you left me, you took everything which I got.

This pain of failure kills me inside. Living without you is like is carrying a piece of iron in my heart. Situations tied me on the bed of thorns. I am not strong enough to escape. You are the one I still desire in the last seconds of my life.

Every time I lock my sights, I fly out to a point where I can sense the warmness of your heavenly embrace.

I tried to stop loving you. So, I built shields around my heart and searched for the other alternatives, if I could replace you, but you carved yourself into my veins.

I will conquer this world if you are with me, I will be on the top of the world, and even the stars themselves surrendered to my fist.

You are a poem of my lifetime. I never knew how to write. You are my story...

Let me kiss you instead and let my lips paint for you all the feelings which I cannot say. I will be waiting for the day where you carry me inside you.

Seeing You

Besides my long looks and far away from the reach of my hand, your gestures are so beautiful – the gestures of love and your presence.

The silence needs to break since I am on the peaks of this world because I kept your magic inside me.

In the colours of sand, nothing around me makes sense, as you continue your conversation with me.

I can't remember how it happened, and I don't know when it will end, but to capture a glimpse of your face, I will hit the earth to the core and make my noise up till Mt. Everest.

Maybe you don't always see it, but you're still inside me when you hurt me. You don't know that you are my only star above the sky.

They say great poets have written their final poem in the most challenging times when left with the pain of separation. It would be great if when I overcome those situations. Finally, I wrote a word that was your name.

End for a Beginning

If everything in this world separates me from you, I will still fight with the infinity to join you. Even my poems are not beautiful enough to tell you how I feel for you. Instead, I will spend the rest of my life searching for a tale which defines you.

Wherever I go, my eyes look for you. The truth that is not having you beside me is tearing me up inside, but I cannot stop thinking about you no matter how hard I try.

Is this very complicated to be with you? Is this the end of everything? Knowing that I can't have you with me keeps me disturbed all the time. Distance is not about living away from you. It is about living with a burning soul.

I was zero when you discovered me – I was aimless, and you showed me the way and given me an ambition. I was an unwanted person, but you completed me. You made me somebody. I was undeserving, but you have made me and given me an honour.

I am myself because of you. Only you can complete me. Today you are not with me, but I carry a lifetime of love that you have given me.

I will love you until God decides that it is time for me to leave this body. Leaving my body is an end, but my love will conquer this world to start a new beginning. In my absence, it will worship you for ages.

www.ingramcontent.com/pod-product-compliance
Ingram Content Group UK Ltd.
Pitfield, Milton Keynes, MK11 3LW, UK
UKHW042001190726
13854UKWH00005B/2102

9 789390 030026